Mockingbird,
Make Up Your Mind!

OGHMA
CREATIVE MEDIA

Bentonville, Arkansas • Los Angeles, California
www.oghmacreative.com

Copyright © 2022 by Victoria Marble
We are a strong supporter of copyright. Copyright represents creativity, diversity, and free speech, and provides the very foundation from which culture is built. We appreciate you buying the authorized edition of this book and for complying with applicable copyright laws by not reproducing, scanning, or distributing any part of it in any form without permission. Thank you for supporting our writers and allowing us to continue publishing their books.

Library of Congress Cataloging-in-Publication Data

Names: Marble, Victoria author/illustrator
Title: Mockingbird, Make Up Your Mind/Victoria Marble |
Description: First Edition | Bentonville: Lee, 2022
Identifiers: LCCN: | ISBN: 978-1-63373-797-6 (hardcover) ISBN: 978-1-63373-798-3 (paperback) | ISBN: 978-1-63373-799-0 (eBook)
BISAC: JUVENILE FICTION/Animals/Birds | JUVENILE FICTION/Imagination & Play
JUVENILE NONFICTION/Science & Nature/Environment

LC record available at: https://lccn.loc.gov/

Lee Press hardcover edition August, 2022

Cover & Interior Layout by Casey W. Cowan
Executive Editor: Chrissy Willis
Editor: Amy Cowan

This book is a work of fiction. Any references to historical events, real people, or real places are used fictiously. Other names, characters, places, and events are products of the author's imagination, and any resemblance to actual events or places or person, living or dead, is entirely coincidental.

Published by Lee Press, an imprint of Young Dragons Press, a subsidiary of The Oghma Book Group.

Mockingbird,
Make Up Your Mind!

Written & Illustrated by

Victoria Marble

LEE
PRESS

an imprint of
YOUNG DRAGONS PRESS

For Emilia and Eric

"A caw, a crow,
a cackle and croon."
A raven cries
by the light of the moon.

Not a black-feathered Raven nor a Crow—
A Mockingbird sings past my window.

Mockingbird, Mockingbird,
where do you go?
Mockingbird, Mockingbird,
how do you know?
Mockingbird, Mockingbird,
each different sound?
Mockingbird, Mockingbird,
show me around!

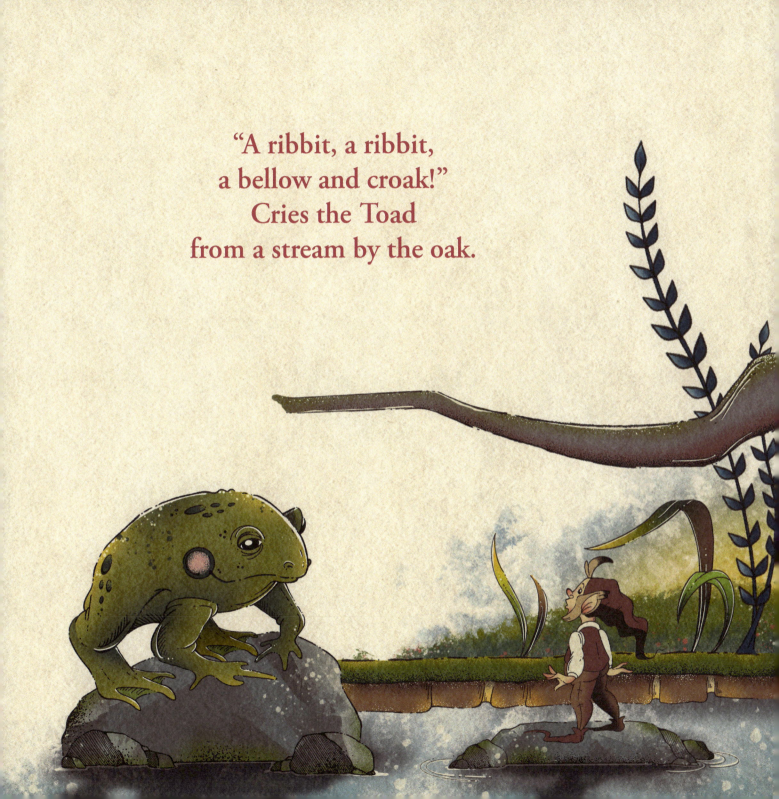
"A ribbit, a ribbit,
a bellow and croak!"
Cries the Toad
from a stream by the oak.

"A ribbit, a ribbit,
a bellow and bog."
Not a Toad nor a Newt
nor a green-bellied Frog

"A ribbit, a ribbit,
a bellow and croak."
My Mockingbird friend
is playing a joke.

Mockingbird, Mockingbird,
what have you found?
Mockingbird, Mockingbird,
what's your next sound?
Mockingbird, Mockingbird,
you can sing on.
Mockingbird, Mockingbird,
song after song.

"A tweet and a twitter,
a twitter-tee-tweet."
The warmth of the sun
makes the Sparrow's song sweet.

"A tweet, a tweet,
a titter and tatter."
It's just the sound
of Mockingbird chatter!

"Chip-a-dee, chirp-a-dee, chirrup-up-up."
A Cricket stirs as the moon comes up.

"Chip-a-dee, chirp-a-dee,
chip-a-dee-dee."
Where is that Cricket?
Where can she be?

"A hum, a hum.
A hoot and a howl!"
Tolls the chilling cry
of a great barn Owl.

"A hum, a howl,
a hoot and a screech."
The Owl naps
on a bough of beech.

Mockingbird, Mockingbird,
now it's all clear.
Mockingbird, Mockingbird,
repeat what you hear!
Mockingbird, Mockingbird,
we've looked around.
Mockingbird, Mockingbird,
what's your next sound?

"A chirp and a croak,
a bellow and croon."
A cackle and caw
by the light of the moon.
"Chip-a-dee, chirp-a-dee,
chip-a-dee-dee!"
The Mockingbird warbles
and whistles with glee.

Mockingbird, Mockingbird, a beautiful choice.
Mockingbird, Mockingbird, you've found your voice!
Mockingbird, Mockingbird, proud as can be.
Mockingbird, Mockingbird, sing more to me!

A Few Words About Mockingbirds....

Growing up near the west coast of California in a suburb of Los Angeles, I recall a number of summer mornings waking up to the boisterous caterwauling of what sounded like several birds in an excited fuss. It was actually a pair of mockingbirds that had nested in our yard.

I remember lying awake one morning listening to a particularly spirited bird rattle on until well past dawn, and I wondered, "Why doesn't he just make up his mind already?" This was the inspiration for *Mockingbird, Make Up Your Mind!*

The sound is probably familiar to many.

The Northern Mockingbird is the only mockingbird species native to North America and can be found in most states and as far North as Canada. If you live in an area near meadows or mowed lawns, low shrubbery, and plenty of shade, you may have heard their call.

What makes the mockingbird special is its ability to learn to imitate sounds from its environment, primarily the calls of other bird species. Fascinatingly though, they are also commonly known to mimic amphibians, insects, barking dogs, and even machinery and car alarms!

This is the point I wanted to truly illustrate with Mockingbird.

A **polyglot** is what we call a person who knows how to speak several languages. The mockingbird's scientific name, *Mimus polyglottos,* references this ability, as they can distinctly mimic several hundred different sounds. John James Audubon wrote of the mockingbird in *Birds of America:* "There is probably no bird in the world that possesses all the musical qualifications of this king of song, who has derived all from Nature's self."

The sound is usually that of a breeding male, either trying to claim or defend territory or impress a female. This he does by darting up in the air, flashing the white patches on his wings, and fluttering back down in a showy display. As a member of the jay family (crows, magpies, blue jays), mockingbirds are highly territorial and will swoop or dart at anything they consider a threat, including people.

Despite that, there was a point in history where their song became so desirable that they became popular caged house pets. Human poaching and capture severely affected population numbers at the time. Since then, the species has adapted and has even spread from contained populations to most areas in North America.

Mockingbirds hunt for insects in wide areas with low, well-kempt grass. If you wish to attract mockingbirds to your area, put out water and a birdfeeder and plant low fruit or berry-bearing shrubs and provide plenty of shade.

Mockingbirds in Pop Culture

To Kill a Mockingbird by Harper Lee
The Hunger Games Mockingjay by Suzanne Collins
American Folk Song "Listen to the Mockingbird"
Lullaby "Hush Little Baby"
King Friday's pet mockingbird on *Mr. Roger's Neighborhood*
Personal symbol of Petyr Baelish in *A Game of Thrones*

About the Author

Victoria Marble

Victoria Marble is an illustrator specializing in character & narrative design, with a particular emphasis on children, animals, insects, & floral designs.

Victoria's love for drawing led her to pursue a well-rounded artistic background with courses completed in a wide range of concepts and media, including drawing and composition, figure drawing, painting, illustration, multimedia, and game design. She holds a general studies associate of arts degree with an emphasis on arts & humanities, as well as an associate of science in electronic game art & design. She became an executive board member of her hometown's art association at the beginning of 2015, where she quickly gained local recognition for her uniquely stylized ink-and-watercolor illustrations. Victoria helps edit and coordinate the association's monthly newsletter in addition to attending meetings and art demos and participating in art shows, galleries, and contests. Her work in the association has won various awards.

Victoria's first illustrated works, *Baum's Wonderful Wizard of Oz* and *Tux in the Zoo* by Diana Aleksandrova, were published by MacLaren-Cochrane in 2019 and 2020 respectively.

Victoria lives in Southern California with her husband and daughter and three little dogs. When not drawing, reading, or writing, Victoria enjoys watching movies with her daughter, eating dessert, and drinking coffee or tea. She is a fan of classical animation, *The Great Gatsby* and the roaring twenties, and Audrey Hepburn films.

Victoria adores creating art that emphasizes the beauty of nature—and particularly birds, fish, insects, and floral designs, along with cute children and animal characters.

CPSIA information can be obtained
at www.ICGtesting.com
Printed in the USA
BVHW021755120822
644473BV00007B/74